SUPER TURBO

VS. WONDER PIG

By Lee Kirby
Illustrated by George O'Connor

LITTLE SIMON

New York   London   Toronto   Sydney   New Delhi

LITTLE SIMON

An imprint of Simon & Schuster Children's Publishing Division • 1230 Avenue of the Americas, New York, New York 10020 • First Little Simon paperback edition February 2018. Copyright © 2018 by Simon & Schuster, Inc. All rights reserved, including the right of reproduction in whole or in part in any form. LITTLE SIMON is a registered trademark of Simon & Schuster, Inc., and associated colophon is a trademark of Simon & Schuster, Inc. For information about special discounts for bulk purchases, please contact Simon & Schuster Special Sales at 1-866-506-1949 or business@simonandschuster.com. The Simon & Schuster Speakers Bureau can bring authors to your live event. For more information or to book an event contact the Simon & Schuster Speakers Bureau at 1-866-248-3049 or visit our website at www.simonspeakers.com. Designed by Jay Colvin. The text of this book was set in Little Simon Gazette.

Manufactured in the United States of America 0118 MTN 10 9 8 7 6 5 4 3 2 1

Cataloging-in-Publication Data for this title is available from the Library of Congress.

ISBN 978-1-5344-1182-1 (hc)

ISBN 978-1-5344-1181-4 (pbk)

ISBN 978-1-5344-1183-8 (eBook)

CONTENTS

1

AN A-MAZE-ING POWER

BEHOLD! SUNNYVIEW ELEMENTARY SCHOOL! INSIDE THESE WALLS THERE IS A BIG SECRET.

SUNNYVIEW ELEMENTARY SCHOOL

But right now, the big secret was . . . how Turbo, official pet of Classroom C, was going to get out of here.

"I feel like I've been this way already," Turbo said, scratching his head. And he was right. He had been this way before—many times, in fact. For you see, Turbo was

1

currently trapped in a maze!

It was too much for a simple hamster to deal with. Luckily, Turbo was anything but a simple hamster.

Because Turbo was really . . . Super Turbo!

What's that? You've never heard of Super Turbo, the world's mightiest hamster? Then, have you never heard of the Superpet Superhero League, of which Super Turbo is a member in good standing? Are you sure? You *must* have heard about all the times he saved Sunnyview Elementary.

Well, those stories will have to wait. The only thing that matters now is: How will our tiny hero get out of this maze?

HE RAN LEFT,

RIGHT,

STRAIGHT,

BACK DOWN,

LEFT AGAIN,

Super Turbo felt like he had run into a big furry brick wall.

"Whoa, are you okay?"

Turbo looked up to see his friend, Angelina, standing over him. She reached out a paw to help him back to his feet.

Like Turbo, Angelina was an official classroom pet—but of Classroom B, instead of C. It was only recently that Turbo had even learned of Angelina's existence, but he liked her a lot. They had so much in common! They were both fuzzy, they both ate food pellets, and they both had pink ears and adorable little noses that liked to twitch.

Of course, as a guinea pig, Angelina was quite a bit bigger than Super Turbo, and was therefore a lot stronger too. She used her superstrength, as well as her uncanny sense of direction, to fight evil as . . .

"Thanks for coming over and helping me train in this maze," said Super Turbo to Wonder Pig. "I think I almost found my way out. I can practically smell freedom!"

YOU'VE BEEN RUNNING AROUND IN CIRCLES FOR THE LAST FIVE MINUTES!

"I have?" asked Super Turbo.

"Yeah, follow me," said Wonder Pig.

A few seconds later, Super Turbo and Wonder Pig exited the maze of books in the reading nook of Classroom C.

"I don't know how you do it," said Super Turbo, looking back. "You always know just which way to turn!"

"It's a gift," said Wonder Pig. "But *every* member of the Superpet Superhero League brings something different and special to the table."

"I guess that's

true," said Super Turbo thoughtfully.

"Yeah, and now you should use *your* special ability to go get us some food pellets!" said Wonder Pig, smiling. "All that maze running has made me hungry."

Super Turbo sprang into action and flew to his cage where his food was kept.

A couple of minutes later he and Wonder Pig were back in the book nook, enjoying a snack.

"I may be good at directions, but you can fly!" said Wonder Pig. "Boy, I'd sure love to try flying. If only I had a cape. . . ."

2

SECRET DELIVERY

The next morning, Turbo was still pretty sleepy from the night before. He and Wonder Pig had accidentally gotten distracted as they put the books from the book maze away. They had stayed up way too late reading a story about pirates and lost treasure. Angelina was a big reader, but all the books in her classroom of first graders had too many pictures and not enough words.

Every morning before class started, Turbo would do a quick survey of Classroom C to make sure everything was in order. And this morning was no different. Turbo ran down the checklist of his classroom:

BOOKS ALL IN ALPHABETIC ORDER? CHECK!

STINKY MAGIC
MARKERS TIGHTLY
CAPPED? CHECK!

Everything was in perfect order, as usual! Turbo climbed back into his cage with time to spare before the bell rang.

In order to keep up his secret identity as just a hamster, Turbo spent the day doing ordinary hamster things. But his mind was on the Superpet Superhero League meeting later that night. On a normal night Turbo, Angelina, and the rest of the Superpets would meet at their secret meeting spot right here in Classroom C's book nook to compare notes about fighting evil. But tonight was not going to be a normal night!

Frank, aka Boss Bunny, had discovered

that Principal Brickford had signed for a giant incoming shipment of Cheezie Doodles! And Cheezie Doodles are delicious!

So the Superpets had unanimously decided to hold that night's meeting in the cafeteria, both to protect the delicious Cheezie Doodles from harm, and maybe, just maybe, to eat a few bags themselves. After all, protecting the school from evil was hard work and they deserved a treat!

With thirty minutes left in the school day, Turbo decided he had just enough time for a little afternoon snooze. *Because a superhero should never be tired and cranky while on the job*, he thought.

Hours later, Turbo woke up to a dark, empty classroom.

Oh no! He must have overslept. Turbo jumped up and hopped out of his cage. Then he sprinted toward the vents that led to the cafeteria.

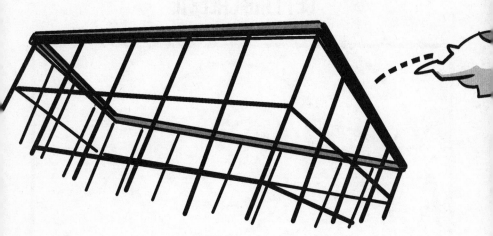

3

GETTING CHEEZIE

As if Turbo weren't late enough, he kept making wrong turns in the vent system. Usually, he ran into Angelina since their class-rooms were so close together. She often led him through the maze to wherever the team was meeting. But tonight he didn't see her. He must be really really late!

When Turbo finally got out of the vent he realized something awful.

In his rush to get to the cafeteria, he had completely forgotten to put on his cape and goggles.

The rest of the Superpet Super-hero League were already huddled together, and of course they were all in their official superhero costumes.

Warren, aka Professor Turtle, turned to look at Turbo. "Oh hey, . . . Turbo," he said. "About time . . . you got here."

CLEVER, THE GREEN WINGER, HAD FLOWN TO THE TOP OF THE PANTRY AND WAS THROWING DOWN BAGS OF CHEEZIE DOODLES.

NELL, THE FANTASTIC FISH, WAS USING HER FISH TANK TO PUSH ALL THE CHEEZIE DOODLES INTO A BIG PILE.

LEO, AKA THE GREAT GECKO, WAS USING HIS WALL-CRAWLING POWER TO DIRECT THE WHOLE OPERATION.

BOSS BUNNY WAS SUPPOSED TO USE HIS SUPER NOSE TO SNIFF OUT TROUBLE, BUT REALLY HE WAS JUST SNIFFING FOR BAGS OF OPEN CHEEZIE DOODLES.

"Hey, has anyone seen Wonder Pig?" asked Turbo, looking around.

"Haven't seen her," came a voice from out of thin air. "We figured she was coming with you."

"Yikes!" yelped Turbo, jumping

onto Professor Turtle's back. "I just heard a g-g-ghost!"

"Don't . . . be silly, . . . Turbo," said Professor Turtle. "There is . . . no . . . scientific proof . . . of the existence . . . of ghosts."

"Yeah, Turbo," said the voice with a laugh.

A green tail suddenly started to appear. Then four green legs. Finally, Turbo realized what—or who—was speaking.

"Penelope!" said Turbo, hopping back down to the ground. "Nice to see you!"

Penelope was
the newest member
of the Superpet Superhero League.
She was so new, in fact, that she
didn't even have a superhero name
yet. What she did have was a
super cool superpower—she could

camouflage by turning any color she wanted!

"That's weird," said the Great Gecko, scurrying down the wall. "It's not like Wonder Pig to miss a meeting."

"Maybe she forgot that we were meeting in the cafeteria," offered Fantastic Fish. "Maybe she went to Turbo's classroom instead."

"Forget food?" laughed Boss Bunny, through a mouthful of Cheezie Doodles. "That doesn't sound like Angelina."

"It sure doesn't," said Turbo, rubbing his chin. But before he could say another thing—

"G-g-ghost!" yelled Professor Turtle,

jumping into Penelope's arms.

4

TUG-O-DOODLE

The Superpets stared in amazement as the bag of Cheezie Doodles slid across the floor! It was The Green Winger who realized what was happening first.

"That's no ghost!" she yelled, swooping down. "The bag's on a line! Someone's dragging it!"

In a rush, the Super-pets ran to the Cheezie Doodle bag and grabbed it. It *was* on a line! Someone had gone fishing and hooked it. And now they were dragging it toward a crack in the wall.

"And I bet I know just who it is," said Turbo. "Whiskerface!"

And he was right. On the other side of the wall, Whiskerface and his

Rat Pack were tugging on the line. Whiskerface was the archenemy of the Superpet Superhero League, and it seemed like anytime anything evil happened in Sunnyview Elementary, he and his rotten Rat Pack were behind it.

"Pull harder!" squeaked Whisker-face. "An extra Cheezie Doodle for the rat who pulls the hardest!"

In the cafeteria, the Superpets yanked on the bag with all their might. Without his super costume, Turbo moved to the back. He didn't want to reveal his true identity to those no-good rats.

"Guys, you can do it!" yelled Fantastic Fish. Trapped as she was in the Fantastic Fish Tank, she could only shout encouragement.

But however much they pulled, the Superpets were losing ground, inch by slow inch. They were out-numbered and just not strong enough. The last corner of the bag was about to disappear through the crack when suddenly—

The pets tumbled back. The Superpets heard squeaky laughter on the other side of the wall.

"Thanks for the snack, Super Pests!" came Whiskerface's mocking voice.

"We'll get you next time!" shouted The Great Gecko, leaping to his feet.

"Boy, we really could have used Wonder Pig and her super strength," said Boss Bunny, dusting himself off.

Turbo gasped. "Maybe the Rat Pack did something to her to get her out of the way!" he said suddenly.

Concerned, the Superpets all raced through the vents toward

Classroom B, where they found . . .

"Oh hey, guys," said Angelina, waving from her hammock. "Yeah, I'm just relaxing. I stayed up too late reading last night."

"You missed the meeting!" said The Great Gecko.

"And the Cheezie Doodles!" said Boss Bunny.

"And we had a life and death struggle with Whiskerface and we lost!" said Professor Turtle, surprisingly fast.

Angelina hopped back into her hammock and gave a mighty yawn. "Sorry I missed the meeting, guys. Like I said, I'm still super tired."

And that was that. Everything was okay, it seemed, so the Superpets each went their separate ways

to their own classrooms. As Turbo
headed back to Classroom C, he
had to admit to himself: Angelina
hadn't sounded very sincere. . . .

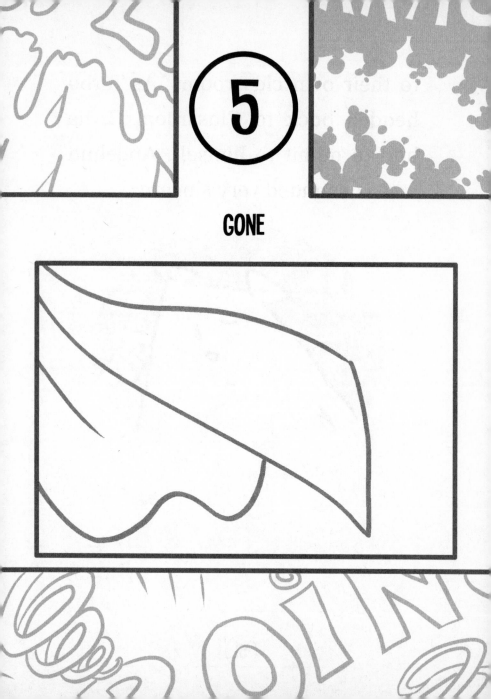

5

GONE

Turbo climbed back into his cage. What a strange night! The Super-pet Superhero League had lost their first battle and Angelina had sure been acting strange. It all made him feel funny.

Luckily, there was always one thing that made him feel

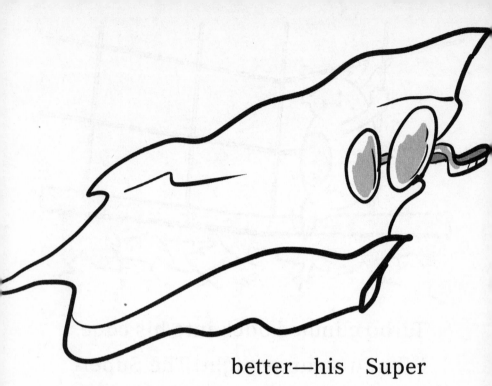

better—his Super Turbo uniform.

Tonight, Super Turbo needs to be vigilant, he thought, and walked over to his food bowl, where he kept his cape and goggles. He lifted the bowl up and—

His super gear was missing! Without his cape and goggles, how could Turbo ever become Super Turbo again?!

Turbo paced back and forth in his cage, thinking hard. Could the Rat Pack have snuck in and stolen his cape and goggles?

But no, that isn't possible, he thought. *The Rat Pack was just in the cafeteria, with me!*

Turbo slowed down and tried to remember the last time he had actually seen his cape and goggles. It had been last night, when Wonder Pig was over. Then Turbo suddenly remembered something Angelina had said.

An icky feeling crept through his stomach. Wonder Pig had seemed awfully keen on his cape, hadn't she? And then she missed the Super-pet meeting and didn't even seem that upset about it. What if . . .

Turbo felt awful even thinking it. But he had to admit, it sort of made sense. Angelina liked his cape, she had missed the meeting, and she was acting strange. And now his supersuit was gone!

Before he even realized what he was doing, Turbo had snuck back into the vents leading to Classroom B, where Wonder Pig made her home.

AS QUIET AS A VERY QUIET MOUSE, TURBO TIPTOED OVER TO ANGELINA'S CAGE.

Turbo peered in, but Angelina wasn't there! Her empty hammock gently swayed from side to side. Clearly she couldn't be that tired if she had left in the middle of the night. What was she up to?

His eyes scanned the rest of her cage. No sign of his cape or goggles. But maybe Angelina had hidden them. Maybe she'd buried them like the treasure they had read about last night. He let himself into her cage and dug around her cedar chips. Nothing.

It could take all night to search Classroom B. A new wave of guilt washed over Turbo. Did he really think his *friend* had stolen his supersuit? He had to head back to his own classroom before Angelina returned and found him snooping. Tired, sad, and confused, Turbo returned to Classroom C.

6

AN EMERGENCY MEETING!

The next day, as soon as school was over, Turbo called an emergency meeting of the Superpet Superhero League. All the pets assembled in the book nook of Classroom C. Even Wonder Pig. Turbo watched her closely, looking for any sign of guilt.

"So, Turbo," said the Great Gecko, "why did you call this emergency meeting?"

Turbo was so busy watching Wonder Pig he didn't notice everyone watching him.

Everyone *except* Wonder Pig. She seemed . . . distracted. *Something must be bothering her,* Turbo thought. And he was afraid he knew what that something was.

He didn't want to accuse Wonder Pig of something she didn't do, though. If she was innocent, his suspicions could ruin their friendship!

"Oh, uh, I was thinking," he began, "about yesterday . . ."

I, UH, THINK WE SHOULD GO DOWN TO THE CAFETERIA. STAND GUARD. MAKE SURE WHISKERFACE DOESN'T TRY TO STEAL THE CHEEZIE DOODLES AGAIN.

BUT WOULDN'T THE CAFETERIA LADY HAVE ALREADY PUT THEM AWAY BY NOW? THERE'S PROBABLY NOTHING TO GUARD.

SHE'S RIGHT. PRINCIPAL BRICKFORD WILL HAVE MADE SURE THE FOOD WAS SECURE.

Now, that's suspicious, Turbo thought. Out loud he said, "At your place? Can we see too?"

Angelina looked up for the first time, right at Turbo. He tried hard to read her expression.

SORRY. IT'S . . . IT'S A SECRET.

A secret? This was too much! Turbo felt like he was going to explode.

"Well," said the Great Gecko, taking charge, "unless anyone has anything else to say, I guess this meeting of the Superpet Superhero League is over."

Everyone started to get up. But not Turbo. He just sat there, trying to decide what to do. It was now or never.

"There is one other thing!" he blurted out. "Last night, while we were fighting Whiskerface, someone came into my cage and stole my cape and goggles!"

"Oh no!" said Penelope. "That's terrible!"

"Who would do such a thing?" asked Fantastic Fish.

"Are you sure you didn't just misplace them?" asked Green Winger.

But Turbo didn't seem to hear any of them. He just looked Wonder Pig right in the eye.

"Oh, I know who would," he said, pointing.

7

THE SIDES ARE DRAWN

All the Superpets let out a gasp at once—all of them except Wonder Pig, who stared at Turbo with a wounded look. For a moment, Turbo felt bad.

"Turbo, what are you saying?" asked the Great Gecko. "This is Angelina, the Wonder Pig! She's our friend!"

Turbo told
his story in a rush. How
the other night Angelina had men-
tioned she would love to fly, and
how much she liked his cape.

"It is a nice cape," said Penelope.

"And flying is pretty awesome,"
confirmed the Green Winger.

Turbo went on, talking about the

battle with Whiskerface, and how Angelina wasn't there. About how strangely she had acted when they went and found her.

"Yeah, it was weird that Angelina wasn't there," said Boss Bunny thoughtfully.

"We could really have used her strength in that battle," added Fantastic Fish.

He told the Superpets about coming home to his cage afterward, and looking in his secret spot for his cape and goggles, and how they weren't there. And when he went to Classroom B in search of them, Angelina was missing from her cage too! The whole time Turbo was talking, Wonder Pig just glared at him silently.

THEN SHE CLEARLY SNUCK OUT OF HER OWN CLASSROOM TO PRACTICE FLYING!

"I can't believe you would even *think* I could do such a thing," Wonder Pig said in a quiet voice.

That sick, sad feeling in the pit of Turbo's stomach came back. But before he could say anything, the Great Gecko stepped forward.

Wonder Pig walked
right up to Super Turbo
and put her pink nose against
his.

"Turbo, I did not take your cape.
And I can't believe you snuck into
my room! If you don't apologize,
I'll . . . I'll . . ."

8

DIVIDED

The thing about Sunnyview Elementary School is that it has a lot of walls. And in those walls, there are a lot of cracks. And in those cracks, there is a lot of room for little tiny rat spies. And it was one of these little tiny rat spies who was running right now to tell Whiskerface what he had just seen.

Seconds later, Whiskerface and his Rat Pack were looking out from a crack in the wall of Classroom C.

Down below, the Superpets were unaware they were being watched. Turbo looked at Angelina. He could

see in her eyes she was upset. How
had it come to this? How could he
have accused his friend of stealing?
He knew what he must do.

WHY, THEY'RE NOT
FIGHTING AT ALL! THEY'RE
JUST STANDING THERE . . .
ANGRILY.

WONDER PIG,
ANGELINA, I AM
VERY—

THIS IS BORING!

WHAT HAPPENED?

SHE POPPED HIM IN THE NOSE! HER MIGHTY FISTS WERE SO FAST I DIDN'T EVEN SEE THEM MOVE!

SUPERPETS, TO BATTLE!

All of a sudden, Classroom C erupted into chaos as Superpet fought Superpet. Turbo couldn't believe it! Angelina had bopped him on the nose! Just as he was about to apologize, too! He ran at her, but she held him at arm's length.

The Great Gecko scampered onto
Fantastic Fish's Fish Tank.

Boss Bunny was using the rubber band from his utility belt to try to peg The Green Winger, but he only succeeded in snapping the rubber band back at his own face.

A short distance away, Penelope and Professor Turtle faced off.

Up on the shelf, overlooking the battle, Whiskerface and the Rat Pack were squeaking with glee.

"Oh, this is the best!" cried Whiskerface, wiping away a tear of joy. "This is even funnier than that time I scared the lunch lady and she tripped and fell into the garbage!"

By now, Wonder Pig had grabbed Turbo by the legs and was holding him upside down. But now that

Turbo was upside down, he had a new perspective on the classroom. And he could see Whiskerface!

"H-H-Hey! L-L-Look!" he yelled out, pointing. "W-W-Whisker-face!"

Wonder Pig dropped Turbo. "That dirty rat!"

The Superpets stopped fighting
all at once. They looked around as
if coming out of a daze. The classroom was a mess and they had

been fighting their best friends. How embarrassing!

The Superpets looked up at Whiskerface.

And with that, Whis-kerface and the Rat Pack scurried away deep into the walls.

"I told you we'd get you next time," yelled the Great Gecko, shaking his fist.

"Yeah, you're no match for us now!" said Turbo, raising Angelina's arm. "Not when we have the Wonderful Wonder Pig back on our side!"

9

LOST AND FOUND

Angelina looked down at Turbo.

"*Are* we on the same side, Turbo?" she asked.

Turbo gulped. That funny feeling in his belly was back, but he knew how to get rid of it.

A superhero knew how to admit when he was wrong.

ONLY, WITHOUT MY CAPE, I DON'T KNOW IF I'LL EVER BE SUPER AGAIN . . .

"Well then, what are we all wait-ing for?" asked Wonder Pig, turning to the other Superpets. "Turbo's super outfit is still missing! We've got to find it!"

THE SUPERPETS
LOOKED HERE,

OVER HERE,

IN THERE,

EVEN HERE.

"I don't get it!" said Penelope, hands on her hips. "Turbo's stuff has disappeared better than I ever could!"

"Think back, Turbo," said Wonder Pig. "Where was the last place you saw everything?"

"Well . . . ," said Turbo, thinking, "it was when you were here, and we were reading a book."

"It was so late I don't remember it that well," Wonder Pig admitted.

"Yeah! It was so late that my eyes

were getting blurry. So I took off my goggles to wipe them clean with my cape—" Turbo stopped and looked right at Wonder Pig. The two of them raced over to the book nook, pulled out the book they had been reading, and—

MY GOGGLES! MY CAPE!

WHEN WE WERE CLEANING UP WE MUST HAVE ACCIDENTALLY COVERED THEM!

The Superpets all gathered around Super Turbo and Wonder Pig, happy that Turbo had found his gear and their friends had made up.

"Hold on a second," said Boss Bunny. "There's still something I'm confused about. Wonder Pig, why did you miss the meeting in the cafeteria?"

"Yeah!" piped in The Green Winger. "And what was the secret thing you had to do?"

Wonder Pig flashed a big, goofy smile.

"Well, I had wanted this to be a surprise . . . be right back!" And then she scampered off into the vents.

10

WONDER PIG'S WONDERFUL SURPRISE

Wonder Pig returned a few minutes later with a curious box.

She held it up proudly and started her tale. "You see, when Turbo and I read about buried treasure the other night, I remembered a rumor I once heard." The Superpets gathered around, eager to hear the story.

"Some-where in this school there is a place where lost treasure magically appears," she continued. "And that place is called: the Lost and Found."

Wonder Pig went on to tell them how she'd decided to go on an adventure and hunt down this treasure, hoping to find something fun to bring back to her friends as a surprise. She had missed the meeting in the cafeteria because she had been busy drawing a map based on the clues that she'd overheard from one of the teachers. Then, late that night, after the Superpets had come to check on her, she had ventured into the halls to find the Lost and Found. And she had!

"And now I have something special for each one of you!"

With a flourish, Wonder Pig lifted the lid off the box and started pulling out items one by one.

PROFESSOR TURTLE, FOR YOU I FOUND A SUPERFAST CALCULATOR.

BOSS BUNNY, HERE'S A SUPER SILLY RUBBER BAND SHAPED LIKE A BUNNY TO ADD TO YOUR UTILITY BELT.

A COMPACT MIRROR FOR THE GREEN WINGER TO HELP HER PREEN.

A BULL'S-EYE PERFECT FOR THE GREAT GECKO'S TARGET PRACTICE.

I FOUND A COLORFUL PIECE OF CORAL FOR FANTASTIC FISH'S FANTASTIC TANK.

PENELOPE, I PRESENT TO YOU A CAMOUFLAGE BANDANA IN CASE YOU EVER GET TIRED OF CHANGING COLORS BUT STILL WANT TO HIDE.

Then, Wonder Pig turned to Super Turbo. "For you, I found something really special," she said as she handed him something small and round.

It was a compass! "Now you'll never get lost in the vents again!" Wonder Pig said proudly.

Super Turbo smiled a big smile. It was the perfect gift and Wonder Pig really was the perfect friend. He knew that he would never again doubt the awesomeness of . . .

THE SUPERPET SUPERHERO LEAGUE!